Disney

TRON
LEGACY

TRON
LEGACY

A NOVEL BASED ON THE MAJOR MOTION PICTURE

Adapted by Alice Alfonsi
Based on the screenplay written by Eddy Kitsis & Adam Horowitz
Based on characters created by Steven Lisberger and Bonnie MacBird
Executive Producer Donald Kushner
Produced by Sean Bailey, Jeffrey Silver, Steven Lisberger
Directed by Joseph Kosinski

DISNEP PRESS
NEW YORK

Printed in the United States of America

First Edition
1 3 5 7 9 10 8 6 4 2
J689-1817-1-10244
Library of Congress Catalog Card Number on file.
ISBN 978-1-4231-3153-3

This book was set in 12 pt. ULTRAMAGNETIC2 Light
Visit Disneybooks.com

PROLOGUE

WHEN SAM FLYNN WAS A LITTLE BOY, his dad, Kevin, told him a story every night before he went back to the office. Kevin didn't work the night shift or anything. He owned a software company, Encom, and he worked there . . . *a lot*.

Sam loved his father's stories because they were almost always about Tron, the hero of the popular video game his dad had invented.

"The Grid is the digital frontier," Kevin would tell Sam. "Add quantum paring, biodigital teleportation, enfoldment, and they have the power to change everything. . . ."

Hold up, Dad, Sam would think. I'm only seven!

Even though Sam wasn't quite old enough to understand everything his dad said, he loved the stories anyway and would always try to follow along.

"I imagined what it looked like inside the computer," Kevin would say to his son. "I kept dreaming of a world I thought I'd never see. Then one day—"

"You got in," Sam finished, always right on cue.

"I got in . . ." his dad would echo.

Sam understood *this* part of the story. His dad had actually gotten into a computer. He'd played the games from the *inside*.

"The world behind the computer screen was more beautiful and more dangerous than I ever imagined," his father would explain. "But with the help of a brave warrior named Tron, I took down the evil Master Control Program. Then I got back out."

The story always ended there. Except for one important night . . .

"I tried to forget the digital world," Kevin informed his son. "But I couldn't let it go. I kept tinkering, and one day I got inside again."

Sam got excited. This part of the story was new!

"It was *my* world, *my* creation," Kevin said. "But I needed help to build a new system, so I created a program that could think. Like me. Like you. I named it Codified Likeness Utility— or Clu for short. But then something unexpected happened. A miracle!"

His father did not go on. Sam pleaded with him to stay home that night. Sam wanted to hear more of the story. But Kevin shook his head.

"I have to go, Sam," his dad said. "We've got to see how the story ends, right?"

Sam nodded, but his eyes were filled with disappointment. Trying to cheer him up, Kevin promised Sam that they would go to Flynn's arcade first thing the next morning. They could play a couple of levels of the games that Kevin had invented: Space Paranoids and, of course, Tron.

"Can we play on the same team?" Sam asked.

"We're always on the same team, kiddo," his father said before stepping out of the bedroom. They were always in it *together*.

But that wasn't true.

That night, Kevin Flynn disappeared. . . .

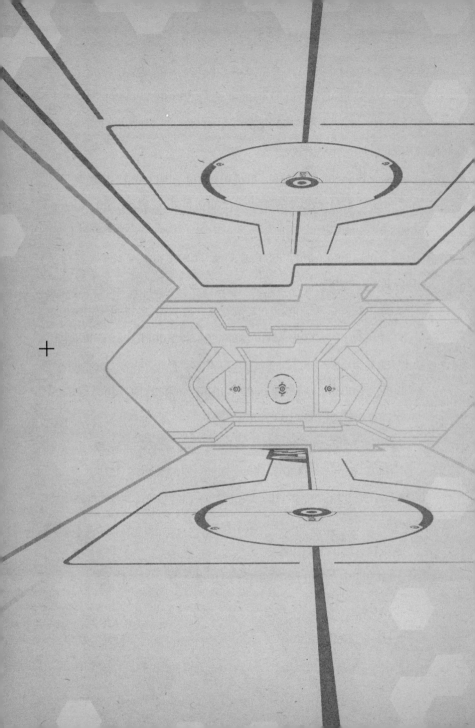

MANY YEARS PASSED, and the pain from his father's disappearance stayed with Sam, refusing to fade. His dad's last words still echoed inside Sam's brain: "We're always on the same team, kiddo."

Sam shook his head angrily, trying to drown out the words. He revved his motorcycle's engine. The wall of noise battered his ears, but the memories would not go away.

Some team we are, Sam thought. I'm here, Dad. I've been here all along! Where the heck are you?

Heat lightning rippled across the night sky. Up ahead, cars hurtled along the freeway. Without warning, traffic slowed to a crawl. Bright red brake lights blinked in the night. Instead of slowing down, Sam sped up, expertly darting his bike around the scarlet lights.

I have to get there on time, he thought. Especially tonight . . .

It was exactly twenty years ago to the day, that Sam's dad had finished his bedtime story, left for the office . . . and vanished.

At the time, Kevin Flynn's disappearance had been front-page news. After all, he owned one of the biggest companies in the world. There was a huge media circus. Reporters camped out in front of Sam's home. But the stories were all about the fate of Encom. No one really cared about young Sam. He was just a kid with a mom who'd died a few years before and a genius dad who'd gone missing—without even saying good-bye.

It's that stupid company's fault my dad is gone, Sam thought. Encom was always more important to Dad than me.

After his father vanished, Sam inherited a huge stake in his company. But Sam didn't care. He pretended the company didn't exist, except on one day every year—the anniversary of his father's disappearance.

Every year on that day, Sam pranked Encom. Once he

performed a flaming motorcycle stunt at the company barbecue. Another year he hacked into the CEO's computer. Then there was the time he bungee jumped during a big press junket.

Sam knew these wild pranks could never make up for a life without his father. But the stunts gave him satisfaction. On that one day a year, he made sure everyone at Encom remembered that he was still here—and that his dad wasn't. It was, in a weird way, his only connection to the father he would probably never see again.

For tonight's very special anniversary, Sam had planned something really spectacular.

Pulling free of his memories, Sam gave a sharp jerk on his motorcycle handlebars and cut across six lanes of traffic. He blew down an off-ramp, ran a red light, and swerved into a narrow alley. Finally, he parked the cycle on a big commercial boulevard. In the daylight hours, these streets were very busy. Now they were dark and deserted. Everyone was home—with their families.

With his backpack slung over his shoulder, Sam jogged toward Encom Tower. In the quiet shadows of the night, a young man joined him. The kid wore a dark hoodie, black jeans, and dark sneakers. This was Sobel. He was an acquaintance of Sam's. Sam didn't have friends.

"You were on time," Sobel whispered gleefully. "That's good. Synchronization is good."

Together, the two jogged to a steel security door near Encom's loading dock. Sam pulled up the cord hanging around his neck. Attached to it was a USB device. He plugged the device into the electronic door lock. Then he connected it to a handheld keypad with a tiny LED screen.

"We take down the big guy up there," Sobel whispered. "That is *assassin* cool. That is rep, bro!"

"Huge rep," Sam quietly replied, still working the keypad.

"But why we always messin' with the same guys?" Sobel asked. "I know they're master-of-the-universe, corporate-evil style, but I want to hit other villains, too. My game is too strong for just one enemy."

"You do have mad game," Sam said halfheartedly, his eyes on the hundreds of cipher codes running through his device. He knew one of them would open the lock.

"You're courageous, Sam," Sobel said. "You're my Butch Cassidy! This is just the beginning!"

Sam noticed something on the screen just then. "Uh-oh . . ."

"What's up?" Sobel asked, worry in his voice.

"They added a new security cipher," Sam explained. "The code I hit . . . I might have just called the cops."

Sobel's eyes grew big. "Cops?"

Sam shrugged. "So we get caught. This is where reps are made, '*assassin*.'"

But now Sobel had gone completely pale. "If I'm caught by the cops, call my stepmom!" He took off down the street. "My stepmom!"

Sam rolled his eyes. Figured. The only person he could rely on was himself. "Okay, Sundance!" he called. See you on the flip side, he added silently.

Just then, the multiple locks clicked, and the security door opened. Sam smiled, tucked the USB device into his jacket, and slung his backpack over his shoulder. Then he took a deep breath and darted through the door.

At the base of the stairs, Sam spotted the red light on the first security camera, indicating that it was active. He slipped a modified laser pointer out of his wrist sheath and fired at the lens.

Somewhere inside Encom, a security monitor went blank. Then another and another as Sam fired at each camera.

Now, that's how we do it, he thought. Invisible people can't get caught.

Sam needed no map as he raced through the building. He'd studied the floor plans and knew exactly which route to take.

After two flights of stairs, Sam arrived at a bank of freight elevators. He hit the button and an elevator instantly opened—just as he knew it would.

Three minutes later Sam stepped onto the skyscraper's roof, his backpack now firmly attached to both shoulders.

The night air was warm and laced with the smell of the ocean. Sam paused in the neon glow of the huge Encom sign that topped the building.

"Hey, Dad," Sam whispered to the dark wind, hoping that wherever his father was, he could hear him asking: "How you doing?"

Just then, Sam heard a heavy door clang. Boots clomped across the roof. Two security guards appeared behind him! It looked like he hadn't been as invisible as he hoped.

Here we go, Sam thought.

A third uniformed man appeared. This last guy was big and beefy. He wore special bars on his collar indicating that he was the guy in charge. "I got you now!" the big man called to Sam.

Sam ignored him as he tugged on the straps of his back-pack, making sure they were secure. Then he began climbing to the top of the neon sign.

The guards shouted at him to get down, but he didn't listen. So the big guard started to follow him up.

Sam kept climbing—right onto a catwalk suspended high above the city. The walkway was attached to a huge crane.

"I've got you cornered," the big officer shouted as he climbed onto the walkway. He faced Sam, moving a step closer.

"Take it easy, buddy," Sam said, backing away.

"The name's Ernie," the guard said. "You should know the name of the sheriff who brought you down."

"You're a *sheriff*?"

"You think you're so smart," Ernie shouted. "Every year at this time, some stupid stunt. And every time with that logo, that *89* symbol you leave behind! But not this year. No more chew-outs from my boss, because *this* year I've got my man!"

By now, the night wind was buffeting them both. The crane began to sway. Sam clutched the rail, looked at the ground far below and then back at Ernie.

"Your boss is fine with this," he informed the man.

Ernie frowned and shook his head. "No way."

"Who's your boss?" Sam asked.

Ernie inched a little closer to Sam. A blast of wind hit them, and the crane's swaying became more violent.

"The security chief is my boss," Ernie shouted.

"That's not actually true," Sam told him, "because your boss works for the board of directors, and they work for the shareholders."

Ernie gave Sam a "so what" look.

"Do you know who the biggest shareholder is, Ernie?"

"I don't know!" Ernie cried. "Some kid!"

Sam stuck a thumb in his own chest—and grinned.

"*You're* the kid?" Ernie groaned.

Sam nodded.

"You're killin' me," Ernie muttered.

Still grinning, Sam dived off the walkway. "See ya, Sheriff!" he shouted as he hurtled toward the pavement.

Ernie looked away, too horrified to watch. That's when he saw the *89* logo glowing from a giant neon sticker now attached to the crane. Sam had struck again.

CHAPTER 2

SAM FELT HIMSELF FALLING FAST THROUGH THE AIR. With a hard jolt, the parachute hidden in his backpack deployed and his body was jerked back up again.

Sam laughed. Everything was working out exactly as planned. He began floating down slowly, his feet dangling over his intended landing zone—the employee parking lot. And then, the gust came.

With a *whoosh* the night wind caught his chute, twisting and turning it.

Uh-oh . . .

While sirens began wailing in the distance, Sam felt the wind sweeping him away from the parking lot. He was drifting helplessly now, over the darkened city streets.

Down, down he floated, and then, with another jolt, he stopped. Aw, no! he thought. His parachute had gotten caught on a streetlight!

Sam looked down to the pavement—the very *hard* pavement. He *could* slip out of the chute's harness and let himself fall to the ground. But it was just a little too high a drop.

With a sigh, Sam folded his arms and waited.

Just then, he noticed a cab rolling down the empty street. Timing his move just right, he slipped out of the parachute harness and landed with a thump on the taxi's roof. *Perfect!*

"Hey, no free ride!" the driver shouted out his window.

Just then, a pair of police cars flew around the corner. Lights flashing, sirens wailing, two more units appeared on the opposite end of the block.

Wow! Sam thought. When I call the cops, I really call 'em!

The taxi was blocked in. The driver hit the brakes. But Sam wasn't stopping. He rolled off the roof of the taxi and landed on his feet. Then he leaped on and over the hoods of both police cars and took off full speed down the street. Behind him, more official vehicles screeched to a halt.

Just as he reached his motorcycle back at the original landing site, a blinding beam of light shone down from above. Sam looked up and saw a police helicopter overhead, its blades beating the night air.

Policemen rushed out of the shadows. They had been waiting. Strong hands seized him. One of the officers snapped a pair of handcuffs on his wrists. Another told Sam what he already knew.

"You're under arrest!"

<< >>

A FEW HOURS LATER, EVERYTHING WAS CLEARED UP. While his dad might not be around, his name still pulled a lot of weight. Uncuffed and released, and not much worse for the wear, Sam left the police station and headed home.

Home for Sam wasn't a nice little ranch house in the suburbs or a huge mansion in a subdivision, which, by the way, he could easily afford. Sam Flynn lived where no one else did, next to a junkyard near the city docks.

During the day, this area was loud and active. Sam didn't

like it much then. But now, just past midnight, the piers were closed, the warehouses were deserted, and the city skyline silently flickered like rows of lit candles in a quiet church.

Sam cut his motorcycle engine and parked beside a stack of boxcar-size shipping containers. Carrying a bag of take-out burgers, he climbed a metal staircase to the container on the very top.

Home sweet home, he thought, pulling out a key.

Thanks to a giant window cut into one side of the metal container, Sam had a great view of the city. But tonight he ignored the scenery.

Walking in the front door, he heard a friendly bark. A furry dog, tail wagging, bounded up to greet him.

"Hey, Marvin," Sam called, reaching into the bag. He tossed his dog a thick, hot burger. "Double-double. No mayo. Just the way you like it."

Marvin barked a thank you and began nibbling on the juicy meat.

Sam went to the fridge and grabbed a cold drink, then headed for the couch with his own burger.

His place was a total mess. Papers and books were

piled everywhere. The shelf was cluttered with rows of action figures, and in the middle of the room, a vintage motorcycle sat up on blocks. This was his father's old bike. Sam was in the middle of rebuilding the twenty-year-old Ducati. One wheel and a lot of engine parts were scattered all over the floor.

Sam stretched out on a couch beside his father's cycle, unwrapped his burger, and began to eat. That's when Sam realized he wasn't alone. A man stepped out of the shadows.

Sam bolted upright in alarm. Then he saw the man's face. "Alan," he said with relief, "what are you doing in my apartment?"

Alan Bradley shrugged. "You don't answer your phone." He smiled. "How ya been, Sam?"

Sam narrowed his eyes. Years ago, Alan had been his father's best friend. After his father had escaped the digital world and focused back on the real world, he'd made Alan a partner at Encom. And when Kevin disappeared, Alan had been the one to help raise the young orphan. Now Alan managed Sam's majority ownership of the corporation—and he *tried* to manage Sam, too.

"When I was twelve I might have appreciated the whole surrogate-father thing," Sam bitterly told Alan. "But come on. I got it under control now."

Alan gestured to the mess around him. "Clearly."

"What is it?" Sam lashed back. "Do you want to help me with my homework?"

Alan turned his back on Sam and peered at the city skyline. "I heard you did a triple axel off the Tower a few hours ago," he said. "Rough landing, huh?"

Sam rubbed the wrists where he'd been cuffed. "Could have been worse."

Alan sighed. "I also heard you sent the last batch of dividend checks to some interesting charities."

"The dog-park thing?" Sam gestured to his canine bud. "That was Marvin's idea."

Alan folded his arms.

"Are we gonna do this again?" Sam asked, shaking his head. "Do I look like I'm ready to run a Fortune 500 company?"

"No," Alan said. "And truthfully, the board's pretty happy with you where you are. That way they can keep doing whatever they want. What I find curious is that annual prank you pull on the company. You have an interesting way of being disinterested."

Sam put down his burger and wiped his hands. "Why are you here, Alan?"

"I promised you if I ever got any information about your dad, I'd tell you first," Alan said. "I got a page last night."

"Still rocking the pager," Sam said, stifling a laugh. Pagers were so old-school. "Good for you," he added.

"The page came from the arcade."

Sam shrugged. "So."

"So, that number has been disconnected for twenty years," Alan said. "Ever since your father vanished."

Sam froze.

"Two nights before your father disappeared, he came to my house," Alan went on. "Flynn said he cracked it. He was talking about genetic algorithms, quantum teleportation. Flynn said he was about to change everything. Science. Medicine. Religion." Alan locked eyes with Sam. "He wouldn't have left that, Sam. And he wouldn't have left *you*."

Sam shook his head. He had heard this before. It didn't change anything. It *couldn't* change anything. "You and I both know he's either dead or chillin' in Costa Rica," Sam said angrily. "Probably both. I'm sorry, man. I'm beat, and I smell like jail. Let's reconvene in a couple of years—"

Before Sam could object, Alan tossed him a metal ring. Instinctively, Sam reached out and caught it. "The keys to the arcade," Alan said. "I haven't gone over yet. I thought you should be the one—"

"You're acting like I'm gonna find Dad sitting there working!" Sam cried. "*Ah, sorry, kiddo, lost track of time for, like, twenty years. . . .*"

The older man nodded, stared at the flickering lights of the city. "Wouldn't that be something?" he said wistfully. Sam felt a momentary pang of sympathy. He wasn't the only one his dad had left behind. Then, before he could say anything, Alan walked out the door.

Left alone again with his dog, Sam found his gaze straying to the Tron-game action figures lined up on his shelf.

For the very first time, Sam noticed something. "What the . . . ?" he whispered, looking harder. The plastic face on the Tron figure looked just like the face of Alan Bradley.

When Sam's dad had been trapped inside the computer all

those years ago, it was Tron who'd helped Kevin defeat the evil Master Program.

Does the digital world my dad created really mirror our world so closely? Sam wondered. The thought stayed with him, like an itch he couldn't scratch.

He stared at the keys in his hand, the keys to the arcade. Suddenly, Sam grabbed his helmet and jacket. Before Marvin had time to swallow the last bite of his double-double, no mayo, Sam was back on the freeway.

CHAPTER 1

AS HEAT LIGHTNING RIPPLED THROUGH THE PURPLE SKY, Sam arrived in front of his dad's gaming arcade. It was three a.m., the streets were deserted, and Flynn's was dark and shuttered, just as it had been for two decades.

Layers of old posters covered the entryway. There were flyers for concerts, movies, basketball games—twenty years of event history. Sam ripped them all away. Using the keys Alan had given him, he unlocked the front door.

A beeping sound reminded him to punch in the alarm code. Sam did, surprised his twenty-seven-year-old brain could still access his seven-year-old self's memory.

The arcade was dark. Even after Sam turned on the lights,

the place felt gloomy. Strange shapes lurked under sheets covered with layers of dust, like the creation on Doctor Frankenstein's lab table.

But Sam knew the only creations lurking under the dusty covers were the ghosts of forgotten video games from the 1980s. Every one of them was an antique. The multiplatform, Internet gamers of the twenty-first century had no use for them.

But not everything in this place was useless. As in Frankenstein's lab, Sam suspected there might be a secret lurking inside the arcade. He just had to find it.

Before he could begin his search, something caught his attention. One game, covered in a sheet like all the others, was up against the far wall. He walked up to it, blew away the dust, and pulled the sheet off Tron. He dug into his pocket for a quarter. Just one game, he thought. For old time's sake.

Suddenly the coin slipped between his fingers and Sam groaned. Dropping down to retrieve it, he noticed scuff marks on the floor. It seemed the Tron machine had been moved—and moved a lot.

Why?

Sam tugged on the game, trying to move it himself. For a moment it didn't budge—and then the whole thing suddenly swung outward. The game was concealing a secret doorway!

As Sam stepped over the threshold, an electronic eye activated the room's power. Lights came on by themselves, and Sam gasped in surprise.

It must be Dad's secret laboratory, he realized, his heart beginning to pound.

Frozen in time, a twenty-year-old pot of coffee sat on a stove in the corner. The leather jacket his dad had been wearing the night he vanished was still draped over a chair. A layer of dust covered everything. Gulping, Sam continued to move around, taking stock.

He saw a map tacked to a cork bulletin board. The map outlined a landmass Sam didn't recognize. His father had labeled it THE GRID.

Computer mainframes lined the walls, and a glass and silicon laser array was placed in one corner. The laser was aimed at a chair and table in the center of the room.

Sam sat down in the chair. Suddenly the table in front of him lit up. Sam brushed away two decades of dust and discovered that it was actually a worktable that controlled the computers surrounding him.

Processors began to hum. Then the screen in the center of the table flashed a question: TRON PROJECT *INITIATE SEQUENCE?* Y/N

Sam pondered the question for two whole seconds before pressing Y.

Instantly, a brilliant blue burst of light washed over Sam. "Ahh!" he cried, blinded by the flash.

For a moment, there was nothing but the bright flash and the heavy sound of Sam's startled breathing. It was as if time had been suspended.

Sam finally opened his eyes. Darkness. He blinked and rubbed his eyes, but it didn't help. All the lights in the room had shorted out.

Reaching out in the pitch dark, Sam felt the surface of the table. There were no running lights on the control panel, no humming or vibrations. It was dead. Sam found a manual reboot switch and activated it.

Nothing. No power at all, not even emergency lighting. Muttering in frustration, Sam felt his way out of the secret lab. He moved through the arcade, which was also pitch dark, and finally stumbled out the front door.

Although it was still dim, at least now he could see. And go home. Enough trips down memory lane.

The night air felt different now, wet, foggy, cooler. Maybe the jump off the Encom building had rattled his brain. Shaking his head, Sam walked over to the streetlight where he'd parked his motorcycle. It was gone.

"What?!"

He glanced around and realized the missing bike wasn't the only strange occurrence. Lots of things were different now. Clouds, stars, even the moon had disappeared. The sky above him looked as black as outer space. Suddenly a crackling flash of lightning rippled across the firmament.

Heat lightning again? he thought. But the weather seemed too cool for that. And since when was lightning *blue*?

Sam's heart was now pumping hard enough to drown out the strange electronic buzzing that was assaulting his ears. He couldn't wrap his head around it. Nothing was as it should be. Even the buildings looked different—blank walls without any windows or doors.

That's when a blinding spotlight pinned him. Sam groaned. The police again? "This has to be a new record," he said out loud.

But this was no helicopter. Looking up, Sam's eyes nearly popped out of his head, and his jaw dropped. Hovering over him was an upside down U-shaped Recognizer—*from the Tron game*! The digital construct was blue-black in color, with orange piping.

I'm inside, Sam realized in shock. I'm *in* Dad's digital world!

The Recognizer hovered overhead, its light probing Sam as if he were a specimen under a microscope.

"Identify yourself, program," a booming, metallic voice commanded.

There was no way he was staying around to answer that question. He had to get back into the arcade. Sam tried to run, but the ground under his feet rumbled. Then the streets sank, transforming into deep canyons that surrounded Sam. In seconds, he found himself trapped on a concrete plateau with nowhere to go.

The Recognizer circled its prey then settled on the lone piece of raised concrete. The machine's two legs straddled Sam. Hatches opened, and four guards—or Sentries as Sam remembered them being called—in blue-black armor and smooth, blank helmets walked out of a hangar and surrounded him.

One of them pointed to Sam. "This program has no disc. Another stray."

The voice was electronic, but not without emotion. Sam sensed disdain, maybe even hatred, in the Sentry's tone. A second Sentry seized his arm.

"Wait!" Sam cried.

The Sentries ignored Sam's pleas. They dragged him into the Recognizer's hangar. The hatch closed, and Sam felt the craft lurch under his feet. He was trapped.

‹‹ ››

ONCE THE MACHINE WAS AIRBORNE, the Sentries finally released Sam. But before he could take even a step, crackles of light energy slammed Sam against a bulkhead. More bands of power restrained his hands and feet.

Sam ceased to struggle when the hangar floor became transparent. What he saw was unbelievable. It was the stuff of his father's stories—but in living color.

The Recognizer was flying over a city that appeared to stretch for a hundred miles in every direction. The craft was dwarfed by impossibly high skyscrapers capped by towering spires that rose against the ebony horizon.

The entire metropolis was laid out in a grid pattern. Sam tracked crackling bolts of energy as they raced between the buildings. Blue plasma traveled beside the streets through canals that flowed along every avenue and boulevard, like a river meandering through the forest.

Those same energy beams roiled in the black sky. In one blazing blue flash of lightning a glassy onyx mountain range in the far distance was revealed.

Dragging his attention back inside, Sam noticed other people in the hangar with him. They appeared dazed and frightened. Some watched the view through the floor, but most seemed disinterested.

"Hey," Sam called out. "Does the name Kevin Flynn mean anything to you?"

"Keep quiet if you want to live," a teenager warned, causing Sam to raise an eyebrow. He'd just been asking a question. Giving him a closer look, Sam saw that the kid wore a weird black bodysuitlike piece of clothing that glowed with lines of rippling energy.

Sam looked back at the rest of the people. "Not the games, not the games, not the games," one person chanted. Curled in a ball on the transparent floor, his eyes were hidden behind trembling hands.

"What's his problem?" Sam asked.

"Shhhh," another hissed.

Sam faced the man and gasped. Half his face had been violently torn away, leaving empty space bound loosely together . . . with wavering pixels!

These aren't human beings, Sam realized with a jolt. The Sentry had said it earlier, he just hadn't been paying attention! These are *programs*! Living bio-digital entities. And the Sentries think *I'm* one of them!

Suddenly, the invisible restraints holding Sam released him. He tumbled to the floor. The Recognizer banked, moving into a landing pattern. Finally the airship docked on a platform high over the city streets.

Sentries dragged Sam outside with the other programs. They were greeted by an intelligence officer in translucent armor. A Judge Sentry, identified with a special symbol glowing on his chest plate, stood next to him.

Without wasting any time, the Judge Sentry began pronouncing sentence on every captured program: "I sentence you to the games. . . . I sentence you to the games. . . . I sentence you . . ." He went from one to the other without hesitation.

Most programs accepted their fate meekly, as if they were already doomed. But some were not as quiet.

"Not the games!" shouted one frightened program. He broke away from the Sentries and ran screaming to the rail. Sam watched in horror as the program hurled himself off the platform to the ground far below.

A moment later, the judge approached Sam.

This was his chance. He had to explain the situation and get out of here. He didn't belong here.

"Look," Sam began to tell the judge, "I know you probably get this a lot. But there's been a mistake. I need to talk to somebody—"

But the judge cut Sam off with a simple pronouncement: "I sentence you . . . to the games."

CHAPTER 4

THE JUDGE HAD SPOKEN. Sam was taken away and tossed into a room with four life-size statues of women. He blinked in astonishment when the beautiful "statues" came to life. They were Sirens from his dad's game! Their white unitards glowed alluringly, and they looked as though they had been carved from pure marble.

"Uh," Sam said, "can somebody tell me what—"

The one Sam assumed was the leader—lifted her finger. The tip glowed with a stark white light. The Siren touched his lips, and Sam fell silent. Then she ran the finger along his chest, and the light cut his clothes away, as if it were a surgeon's scalpel.

"Whoa!" Sam protested.

The Siren ignored him as two others returned bearing form-fitting armor. They touched the plates to Sam's legs, torso, and arms. The armor clung to his flesh as if magnetized.

Then the Siren raised her glowing finger again.

"This can't be good," Sam said.

She ran her finger along Sam's armored joints, sealing them and trapping him inside. Arcs of plasma surged through the plating. Sam's newly electrolyzed flesh tingled.

Finally, another beautiful Siren approached Sam. She carried a circular metal disc the size of a dinner plate. Silently, she inserted the disc into a groove on the back of Sam's armor.

Sam's head felt like it was going to explode. And rightfully so. Unbeknownst to him, a powerful processor inside that disc had begun downloading the contents of his mind.

"Mirroring complete," the disc Siren droned. "Disc activated and synchronized. Proceed to the games." She stepped back into the shadows and froze, statuelike once more. The two others joined her, and all three became motionless again.

Sam faced the head Siren. "What do I do?" he asked.

For a moment, it looked as though she might be sympathetic,

as though she might actually help Sam get out of this waking nightmare. But then she spoke. Her answer was one word: "Survive."

A door opened and the floor moved, carrying Sam forward and then straight up a dark chute. He rose and when he could see again, he was in the middle of a vast arena.

Looking around, Sam realized he was standing on a raised platform—one of eight. The platforms were huge circles. Each was separated by a deep abyss. Sam looked down into the black pit beside him. He couldn't see the bottom.

Thunderous applause greeted Sam's arrival. Scanning the arena, he saw thousands of programs sitting in the stands. They weren't just clapping for him. They were clapping for all the contestants—and there were sixteen of them.

The competing programs eyed one another. Some seemed used to their surroundings, and Sam guessed they were veterans of the games. His suspicions were confirmed when those programs dropped into a crouch, waiting for play to begin. The frightened newcomers, on the other hand, shifted nervously. Sam quickly mimicked the seasoned players and dropped into a crouch, too.

Just then, a robotic voice boomed: "The Leader has signaled the start of the games."

Leader? What leader? Sam thought.

Cheers erupted from the audience, and Sam focused. Across the court, his opponent pulled the disc from the back of his armor. A helmet immediately formed over the program's head, and then a visor covered his face, making him battle-ready.

"Yo!" Sam called, realizing the opponent looked familiar in his gear. "I have a three-inch version of you on my action-figure shelf!" Maybe fighting him would be as easy as playing with toys.

Maybe not.

The disc in the progam's hand began to glow. Then the program hurled the disc so fast it singed Sam's hair. Without missing a beat, the disc returned to the thrower's gloved hand like a high-tech boomerang.

The game was officially on. And Sam needed to stay focused.

Just then, a big, bearded opponent threw a disc. But this one wasn't aimed at Sam. This disc was heading for the terrified program on the platform at Sam's right.

The glowing disc hit the quivering program square in the

chest. It exploded into thousands of tiny squares that bounced across the court like shattered glass.

"Program three derezzed," the robotic announcer calmly declared.

Sam swallowed hard. He was freaking out now, but he refused to show it. I can play this, he told himself. Plus, I can't derezz . . . I don't think.

Taking a moment to get his bearings, it occurred to Sam that he had an advantage. He had played a game just like this before—Tron! First level. Single-elimination round.

I can beat this level. I've done it already.

Sam reached behind him for his disc, but it stuck in its sheath. Uh-oh. His opponent threw again. Sam ducked just in time and finally freed his own weapon.

"All right, here we go," Sam said, as the visor instantly closed over his face. Now *he* was battle-ready! He fired his disc.

His opponent dodged Sam's throw and tossed again. This time the disc hit the platform, shattering it under Sam's feet.

Sam yelped as he fell. With one hand he managed to grab the crumbling edge. He caught his returning disc with the other.

"So that's how it is," Sam muttered, pulling himself back up.

His opponent made a huge leap, jumping right onto Sam's broken platform. Standing over him, the program raised his glowing disc like an ax.

"I don't think so!" Sam slammed down his own disc, striking the platform at his opponent's feet. The platform shattered, and Sam's opponent fell into the black abyss.

"Program nine in the pit," the announcer declared.

Shaken, Sam dropped to one knee. He was safe for a moment.

Suddenly his platform moved until he was facing off against the big, bearded gamer, the one who'd derezzed that terrified program.

"Hey, wait!" Sam called. "Can I get a time-out?"

The bearded program charged, letting out a guttural scream.

Forget this! Sam thought. He took off, running across the platform. Ducking the bearded program's throw, Sam slid to the edge of the platform and slipped off!

Hanging over the edge, Sam saw another platform shifting just below him. This was his chance. He let go, falling through the air, just as he had at the Encom Tower—only this time without a parachute.

Sam landed hard, banging into the platform. The program already there looked over. It was a fatal error. Distracted by Sam's arrival, the program was instantly blown apart by a foe.

"Program seven derezzed," the announcer said.

The bearded program leaped after Sam and gave chase. Sam scrambled to get away.

Just then, Sam realized the other platforms were moving closer and closer. Finally they banged together, fusing into one massive gaming court. The arena lights lowered.

This was the final contest. It was Sam versus the big, bearded, angry program.

‹‹ ››

HIGH ABOVE THE ARENA, the Rectifier hovered like a menacing moon. On the bridge of the airship, the Leader sat slumped on his throne.

Dozens of view screens filled the bridge. Each broadcasted a different angle of the games. But the Leader showed little interest in the fate of the programs. The dramatic images fluttered past his gaze like so much pixilated confetti. He had seen it all—many, *many* times before.

With the Leader's features hidden behind a mask, not even Counselor Jarvis knew whether he was watching the screens. Then Sam derezzed the bearded giant, and the Leader sat up and leaned forward.

Jarvis noticed his master's sudden interest. Curious, he turned to an Intelligence Sentry. "What is that program?" Jarvis asked, pointing at Sam.

With his attention trained on Sam, the Leader shifted two black balls in his gloved hand. Jarvis noted the move. That single, innocent signal triggered the entry of a deadly new contestant.

"Rinzler has entered the arena," the announcer informed the crowd.

As cheers went up, Sam watched the sleek, black-armored Rinzler enter. The face of this warrior program was completely hidden behind a dark visor. He drew his disc, and it instantly transformed into *two* metal weapons.

"Come on!" Sam shouted. "Is that even legal?"

Rinzler threw with both hands. The discs closed in on Sam. He leaped at the last possible second, and the discs careened off each another.

A warning siren wailed. A hologram of a giant arrow appeared above Sam's and Rinzler's heads. Then it began to turn. Amazingly, the gravity in the arena shifted with it!

Helpless, Sam felt his body crashing against a translucent dome that now covered the entire arena. Rinzler was dropping on him. He tried to get out of the way, but there was nothing he could do.

Sam cried out as Rinzler's boots landed on his forearms and one of the discs sliced his skin. Pinned, he was helpless as Rinzler raised a disc for the killing blow.

Just then, a drop of blood oozed from the wound in Sam's arm. The globule leaked through a crack in his armor. Beading like mercury, the single drop hung in the air for a moment before dripping, then bursting like a scarlet balloon.

Seeing the blood, Rinzler froze in midstrike. Confused, he lifted his visor-covered face toward the Rectifier overhead.

In answer, a voice boomed out. "Identify yourself, Program."

The electronic voice was not the announcer's. It was Counselor Jarvis who'd spoken.

"I'm not a program!" Sam called in reply.

Another voice spoke, one that sounded oddly familiar to

Sam. "This is your Leader," the man said. "Identify yourself."

"My name is Sam Flynn!"

The crowd began to murmur.

Up in the Rectifier, the Leader turned to Jarvis. This was interesting. Very, *very* interesting.

Below, Rinzler stepped back as two Sentries appeared. Lifting Sam to his feet they led him off the combat court. Then sheathing his deadly discs, Rinzler followed.

CHAPTER 5

THE SENTRIES DRAGGED SAM up to the command bridge of the Rectifier. They tossed him to the deck in front of their master's throne.

Sam glanced around. "Where am I?"

The Leader walked up to Sam. Activating a switch on his helmet, his dark mask dissolved, revealing his face.

Sam staggered backward. He couldn't believe his eyes. It couldn't be. . . . "Dad?" he croaked.

Sam was staring at his father, who looked exactly as he had when Sam last saw him twenty years ago.

The Leader smiled. "Sam! Look at you. Look at the size of you. How did you get in here?"

Sam felt numb. He swallowed. "I got your page," he whispered, "and . . ."

"So, it's *just* you?" the Leader asked pointedly.

Sam nodded. "Yeah. Just me."

"Just you!" the Leader said, sounding relieved. "Wow. This is something, isn't it?"

Now it was Sam's turn to become suspicious. How could twenty years have passed without his father aging a day. "You look . . . the same, Dad."

"But a lot's happened, Sam," the Leader explained. "More than you could ever imagine." He extended his hand. "The disc."

Sam winced as Rinzler yanked Sam's disc from the sheath on his back and handed it to his master. The Leader opened the disc and gazed into it, as though reading a book. Sam watched as billions of bits of information about *his* life were downloaded into the Leader.

"Got it," the Leader said, looking up. "But I expected more."

"You were trapped here. Is that what happened?" Sam asked.

"That's right," the Leader replied vaguely.

"But you're in charge?" Sam said, puzzled. "So we can get out of here now, right?"

der shook his head. "Not in the cards, Sam. Not

"Why not?" Sam asked. "I'm your son!"

"Oh, that." The Leader placed his hand on Sam's shoulder. "You see, Sam. I'm not your father. But I *am* very, very happy to see you."

Not my father? How could that be?

Suddenly Sam put it all together. The Leader looked like his father because Sam's dad had *created* him to look the same! The Leader was really that very special program called—

"Codified Likeness Utility," Sam breathed. "You're . . . *Clu*."

Clu smiled slyly and nodded as if to say, "at your service."

Sam's shoulders sank. Just when he thought he had found his father. . . .

"So," Clu said, grinning. There was a wicked gleam to his eye that Sam couldn't help but notice. "You like bikes, Sam?"

Just like that, the Rectifier lurched and plunged downward. Before Sam could react, Sentries grabbed him again. They dragged him back to the ship's hangar. Clu and Jarvis followed.

The ship landed in the center of the sprawling game grid.

The hangar's bay doors opened, and a long, red-carpeted ramp slid out.

Jarvis descended the ramp first. A moment later Sam and the guards followed.

"Greetings, programs," Jarvis began, his voice filling the arena. "What an occasion we have before us. Today we have a *user* in our midst. For the first time since our liberation!"

The crowd cheered.

Sam's heart beat faster. *User?*

"Better still," Jarvis continued, "this particular user happens to go by the name of *Flynn*!"

The crowd stopped cheering. For a moment, they went silent. Then they began to boo and catcall.

Why? Sam thought. What did my father do? Why do these programs hate the name Flynn so much? But if they hate him, they had to also know him, right?

"Who better to battle this user?" Jarvis asked the crowd. "Perhaps someone who's had experience in these matters . . ."

At that moment, Clu strode down the ramp, a glossy black cape flowing behind him. The cheers began again. And over that wall of noise, Sam could hear Jarvis still chattering on.

"Yes, programs. Your luminary. Your leader. The one who vanquished the tyranny of the users so many cycles ago. I give you . . . Clu!"

As Clu passed Sam, he smirked. "Sorry about your dad, kiddo."

Sam couldn't contain his rage. This *thing* was nothing like his dad. He reached for Clu, but the Sentries restrained him.

Clu raised his arms, basking in the crowd's adoration. "I wonder," he said, "would this user allow me the honor of a challenge?"

Sam's eyes narrowed. "You want to play, Clu? I'll play."

Jarvis stepped forward and opened an ornate box. Two glowing batons rested inside. Clu chose the yellow stick, and Jarvis handed the white one to Sam.

"What do I do with this?" Sam asked, waving the white baton like a sword.

"Not *that*," Jarvis replied with no compassion.

A section of the floor opened, and four gaming programs rose up. Sam didn't know the purple, green, or yellow combatants. But he recognized the teenager holding the aqua baton. It was the young program he'd first seen on the Recognizer, the one who had warned him to keep quiet. This, it would seem, was his team.

A loud whine drew Sam's attention. Two Sentries in silver gray Light Cycles raced toward him.

"You've got no chance, user," the purple program told Sam with a sneer.

"Their cycles are faster than ours," the green program warned.

The Sentries blew by the gamers a second later. Their Light Cycles left a pair of neon light walls in their wake.

Then, as Sam tried to get his bearings, Clu shed his cape and jumped. In midleap, the baton in his hands transformed. It became a black Light Cycle—like a motorcycle that encased Clu's entire body. It was as if Clu had become one with the bike.

With a powerful whine, Clu raced off.

"Now this I can do!" Sam cried, leaping. He squeezed the baton.

When he hit the Grid surface, Sam found himself encased inside a two-wheeled Light Cycle. Beside Sam, the other colors jumped into their vehicles. Together, they roared off after their opponents.

Purple easily caught up with the Sentries—too easily, as it turned out. One Sentry zigzagged across the Grid lines, leaving a barrier of solid light in Purple's path.

Too close to veer away, the purple program struck the barrier and derezzed instantly into bouncing glasslike cubes. Sam zoomed through Purple's debris a half-second later.

Those walls of light are lethal, Sam realized.

Another Sentry tried the same trick on Sam. But seeing a ramp to his side, he cleverly swerved down it.

Clu took the corkscrew ramp at high speed. The yellow program tried the same maneuver, but he crashed and shattered. Sam's team was falling apart!

On the lower level, Sam felt a thump. The first Sentry had found a ramp, too, and came down right beside Sam. Another Sentry closed in from the rear. They were trying to sandwich Sam between them.

As the Sentries tried to squeeze Sam, he aimed for another ramp ahead. Just like on the freeway back in his own world.

Sam shot forward, losing the Sentries. But then he noticed another Sentry closing in on the aqua program.

Sam tried to help the young program. He zoomed off a grid

line, and his Light Cycle shot into the air. Aiming his back wheel, the Sentry crashed into the wall of light left behind. *Smash!*

The aqua bike surged forward! Sam had saved his teammate!

He hit a corkscrew ramp. Two more Sentries appeared and tried to cut him off. But Sam outsmarted them, and they smashed into one another!

Now Sam was catching up with the aqua program.

"We've got to work together!" he called out.

The aqua program nodded.

"Okay, follow me," Sam said.

Racing forward, Sam caught up with another Sentry. Aqua moved to flank their foe, but the Sentry bumped Aqua and he spun out.

Aqua's Light Cycle shattered like glass, but the program was thrown safely clear. Proud that he survived, Aqua raised his arms in triumph.

Clu saw that the young program was off his Light Cycle. Revving his own cycle, Clu shot down a ramp and struck the teenager head-on. The kid instantly derezzed.

No! Sam thought. But he barely had time to react. Clu had skidded into a full circle and revved his engine. A moment later he shot forward, bearing down again—this time on Sam.

Above the whine of the Light Cycle's power processors, Sam could hear the audience cheering.

I'm the last one left, Sam realized. It's him or me now!

Sam kicked his Light Cycle up to full speed and took aim. With the crowd cheering and shouting, Sam made a final, suicidal charge at Clu.

Clu raised his disc for the deathblow.

Sam freed his own disc, its deadly sharp edge gleaming in the blue-black light.

Something else was gleaming, too. Out of the corner of his eye Sam saw a vehicle burst out of a hidden ramp. He recognized it immediately.

"A Light Runner," Sam whispered in awe. It was the bonus vehicle from the final level of the Tron game.

The Light Runner had a razor-sharp nose that cut through the Grid as it moved, splintering it. Behind the Light Runner, a path of rock-hard crystals created a deadly wake.

Sam watched the Light Runner cut right in front of Clu's cycle. Clu tried to swerve, but it was too late. His cycle struck the runner's crystal wall and exploded into spiky shards.

Clu bounced helplessly across the Grid, with bits of his armor breaking off as he flew.

The crowd gasped.

The Light Runner circled Sam and halted beside him. A hatch opened.

"Get in," a voice told Sam.

Sam didn't know what to do. He looked inside the hatch and saw a driver behind the controls. But he couldn't see through the driver's dark visor.

"Get in . . . *now*," the driver insisted.

With no better choices, Sam collapsed his Light Cycle back into a baton. He leaped into the Light Runner's cabin and settled down beside the driver. The hatch closed, and the vehicle made a 360-degree turn.

Across the Grid, Clu got back on his feet as the Rectifier settled to the ground beside him. Jarvis walked down the ramp.

"Flynn lives," Clu told his second, his voice full of barely contained fury—and worry. "It has begun."

Jarvis waved a thin hand, gesturing for the pursuit cycles to get moving. With a thundering roar, the black cycles raced after the Light Runner.

CHAPTER 6

INSIDE THE LIGHT RUNNER, Sam's breathing returned to normal. Turning, he faced the masked driver. "I had Clu right where I wanted him," he complained.

"Clearly," the voice replied. The tone was skeptical.

"Who are you?" Sam demanded.

The driver ignored the question and warned Sam to hold on. By now, a speeding pursuit cycle had caught up with them. Sam felt a jolt as the Light Runner slammed the other speeder.

The pursuit cycle flipped over and derezzed.

It wasn't enough. More pursuits drove through the jagged shards of the first. Among them, Sam saw Rinzler, the dark warrior program who had battled him in the arena.

The driver tapped a control on the console. The button released explosive mines from the belly of the runner. Bombs fell one after another into the path of the pursuit cycles. One derezzed instantly, then another, then a third. Others were coming, but Sam soon realized he was facing a more dangerous threat. Their Light Runner was on a collision course with the Grid's boundary wall! They were going too fast. And the driver showed no signs of stopping!

"Slow down!" Sam yelled. "You can't—"

At the last possible second, the driver punched another button on the control panel. Two electric blue missiles fired from tubes in the hull. They blew a massive hole in the wall!

A split second later, the Light Runner roared through the opening.

"Made it," the driver said, finally retracting the dark visor. "I'm Quorra."

Sam blinked, surprised by the raven-haired beauty who was looking at him. Not what I expected, he thought. But who am I to complain? Behind them, the pursuit cycles skidded to a halt—except for the one that slammed into the wall.

"They're giving up," Sam said.

"Not by choice," Quorra replied. "They can't go off the Grid. They'll have no power."

That's when Sam realized the Light Runner was running without any Grid power. He saw no plasma lines on the topography around him, no glowing strips of power to tap into.

It was hard to believe. From what he gathered, and from stories his father had told him, everything else in this digital world needed the Grid's power. But not the Light Runner. It was running off an independent power source.

"Where are you taking me?" Sam asked.

"Patience, Sam Flynn," Quorra said with her eyes still fixed on the road. "All of your questions will be answered soon."

Sam decided to take her advice. He didn't even flinch when they headed right for the stark stone face of a black granite cliff—and through a secret door that opened automatically.

The Light Runner stopped inside a dark, imposing hangar cut out of solid rock. Quorra led Sam across the hangar and into a sealed chamber. Wall-to-wall windows at the front of the room made it clear that the chamber was perched on top of a mountain peak.

The room was huge and lit with flickering candles. Sam could see the Grid in the distance. It was like looking at a glowing, radiant city through the tall, arched windows of a skyscraper.

The sole occupant was silhouetted against the Grid lights. He sat cross-legged in the center of the massive space, his back to them. The man didn't stir, even when Sam and Quorra's steps echoed on the polished floor.

"Wait here," Quorra whispered.

She quietly approached the man. But before she touched his shoulder, he spoke. "Quorra?"

"Yes?" she replied.

"I'm guilty."

She frowned. "Of what?"

"I finished all the Jin Hua tea," the man said. "I'll brew a fresh pot."

"We have a guest," Quorra said.

The man stretched out his long legs. His feet were bare. Sam thought he saw a beard under the unruly, gray-streaked hair.

"There are no guests, Quorra," the suddenly familiar voice replied. Then the figure rose and faced Sam.

Kevin Flynn.

Father and son stood silently, in awe of each other.

"Sam?" Kevin's voice broke with emotion. "Long time."

"You have no idea," Sam replied. He gazed at the man before him. He was older now. Bearded and tired. But he was definitely Dad.

Kevin walked forward and touched Sam's shoulder, as if to reassure himself that his son were real. "You're here. You're really here."

Sam nodded. "I'm here."

"You're big." Kevin observed the obvious.

"Six-one," Sam replied. "And you're . . . *old*."

Kevin laughed. "How did you get here?"

"Well, Alan Bradley came over," Sam explained, weirded out by how normal this all seemed. "He got your page. Then I found your secret lab in the arcade."

"The pager! Of course," Kevin said, as if he'd just figured something out.

"Clu had him on the Light-Cycle grid," Quorra told Flynn. "I intervened."

Kevin thanked her with his eyes. Then he crossed to the door. "Dinner is soon," he said. "We'll continue our talk then. . . ."

Sam watched his father walk out the door.

"He's strange," Sam said.

"Flynn never thought he'd see you again," Quorra explained.

Same here, Sam thought, but he said nothing.

His gaze traveled to a Light Cycle parked in the corner of the room. Sleek but retro, the machine was ready to rock.

"Vintage," Quorra explained. "Flynn built it many cycles ago for the games. It doesn't get out much these days, but it's as fast as anything on the Grid."

Another corner of the massive room had been turned into a library. A table in the center of the space was occupied by an inlaid chessboard with carved stone figures.

But there were differences from the game Sam knew. He didn't recognize all the pieces, and the board had squares of three colors.

"Looks easy," Sam joked.

"Like chess, but much more complicated," Quorra said. "We're nine years into this game."

Sam gestured to the books.

"Flynn shared them with me," Quorra said. "I've read them all."

Sam scanned the titles. "Light reading. Tolstoy. Chaucer.

Trungpa." He froze on a title. "*Journey Without Goal*? Must have a killer ending."

"Flynn is teaching me the art of the selfless," Quorra explained. "How to remove yourself from the equation."

Quorra leaned close to Sam. "Between you and me, Jules Verne is my favorite," she whispered. "Do you know Jules Verne, Sam Flynn?"

"Sure," Sam replied.

Quorra's eyes lit with interest. "What's he like?" she asked.

CHAPTER 7

IN THE LONG SILENCES DURING DINNER, the silverware clanked inside the massive space. The banquet hall itself was as large as the reception room. It had the same tall windows, and pretty much the same view of the flickering Grid.

A huge fireplace held a bonfire-size digital blaze that lit the room in an *almost*-natural glow.

The table seemed as long as a city block. Enough food to feed a hundred guests was spread out on the white tablecloth. But the only ones dining were Quorra, Sam, and his father.

"You digging the wine?" Kevin asked Sam. "My own special sauce. Never thought we'd have occasion to crack it, but here we are. . . ."

Sam warily lifted his glass. They all sipped.

"You getting the black cherries?" Kevin asked.

"I'm getting more of a motor-oil vibe," Sam said.

"Cool," Kevin said. "I'm getting closer then."

Sam blinked, realizing what his father's words meant. His dad had created everything in this digital domain—right down to the smallest detail, even the wine in their glasses.

"How old are you now, Sam?" Quorra asked.

Sam and his father both replied: "Twenty-seven."

Quorra cocked her head. "Did you attend college?"

Sam nodded.

Kevin started to grin at that until Sam added, "Before I dropped out."

Kevin frowned. "How about work?" he asked his son. "Are you doing anything at Encom?"

"I, uh . . ." Sam shrugged. "I check in once a year."

"Okay," Kevin said, not hiding his disappointment. "Wife? Girlfriend?"

"Dog," Sam said. "Name's Marvin. He's a rescue."

His father nodded. "Dogs are cool."

After a long silence, Kevin met his son's eyes. "I imagine

SAM FLYNN

Alan Bradley received a mysterious message from Flynn's arcade—which has been closed for twenty years.

At the arcade, Sam hopes to find out more about his dad's disappearance.

Sam finds his father's secret laboratory hidden behind the video game Tron.

Sam's not in the real world anymore—he's in the Grid.

Beautiful Sirens help prepare programs—and Sam—for the games.

Armed with a special disc, Sam must react quickly or risk being derezzed.

QUORRA

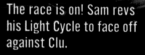

The race is on! Sam revs his Light Cycle to face off against Clu.

Kevin Flynn's secret hideout is tucked away deep in the Outlands. Will Sam find answers there?

KEVIN FLYNN

you have a lot of questions," he said.

"Actually, just one," Sam replied.

His dad sighed, already guessing. "Why I never came home?"

Sam nodded.

Kevin rose and gazed through the window. "Those nights, when I went to the office, I was really coming here," he confessed. "At first it was about the games. But it quickly became about much more. . . ."

Kevin faced Sam and Quorra again. "I realized this was a place of infinite possibilities," he said. "But I couldn't be here all the time. I had you, Sam. I had Encom. I needed partners to help out—"

"Tron and Clu," Sam said.

Kevin nodded. "We were building a whole new world. And just when I thought it couldn't get any more profound, something unexpected happened—"

Sam recalled the conversation the night his dad had vanished. "The miracle?" Sam asked.

"The miracle," Kevin replied. "Isomorphic algorithms. ISOs for short. The next step in evolution. If my coming here to the digital realm was a small step in mankind's evolution, then the ISOs were a giant leap."

"And you created them?" Sam asked.

Kevin stared into the fireplace. "No. They simply manifested, like a flame. They weren't really from anywhere. The conditions were right, and they came into being."

Kevin's bearded face seemed suspended in the glow of the fire. "It was humbling," he said. "Any program I wrote would inherently have my flaws embedded in it. But the ISOs—they were like flowers sprouting in a wasteland. They were individual. Creative. They had free will. As soon as I saw them, I knew this was why I came here, to build a world where they could be born into, then somehow bring their special gifts back to our world. The endless possibilities of their root code—their digital DNA—is spectacular. All I needed was time. . . ."

"So what happened?" Sam asked.

"Clu happened," Kevin said with a frown. "What I saw as a miracle, Clu saw as a virus. An imperfection. Clu took over. Staged a coup."

Kevin's frown deepened. "Clu tried to have me derezzed. But Tron helped me escape."

"What happened to Tron?" Sam asked.

"The Black Guard captured him that day," Kevin said sadly.

"I think Clu destroyed him. Whatever the case, I never saw Tron again. I fled the city, to this safe house I had secretly constructed in the mountains. I saw the light over the city go dark as the Portal closed. . . ."

Kevin turned away from his memories of that terrible time.

"Sam, I *tried* to come home," Kevin explained, his voice earnest. "But the Portal shut down on me. As a fail-safe, I'd set the door to open only from the outside, and only for a limited time. During the chaos after Clu's takeover, it closed. That was the last night I ever saw you."

"Clu thought you'd forgotten your mission?" Sam asked.

Kevin nodded. "He knew that this great experiment of the Grid was just that—an experiment. Clu also understood that the ISOs were a breakthrough. They were the future, and Clu wasn't."

Sam shook his head. "Why didn't you fight?!"

"He did," Quorra quickly replied.

"Clu fed on my resistance," Kevin explained. "The more I fought, the more powerful he became. His first act was the elimination of the ISOs."

"The Purge," Quorra said.

Sam swallowed hard. "Clu killed them all?"

Kevin's expression turned grim. "It was genocide."

They sat in silence for a long time. Then Kevin led Sam and Quorra onto a veranda.

"So," Sam said, taking in the view, "if the Portal was activated when I came in, it must be open now."

His father nodded. "For a time, yes."

"So we can go. *Home*," Sam said. "We make a run for it, get you out of here."

"Sam, don't rush," his dad cautioned.

"What do you mean?" Sam cried. "The Portal. It's going to close!"

Quorra tried to explain. "The moment Flynn is on the Grid, Clu will stop at nothing to obtain his disc."

"My disc is everything, Sam," Kevin said. "The master key. The golden ticket. The way out, and not just for me—"

"What do you mean?" Sam asked.

"With my disc, it's possible for Clu to escape, too," Kevin said. "Our worlds are more connected than anyone knows. Clu figures if I can get in—"

"He can get out," Sam concluded. "And what then?"

"Game over for our world," Kevin said. "Clu doesn't dig imperfection."

Sam threw up his hands. "So that's it? We do nothing? We just sit here?"

Under his beard, Kevin's lips curled into a smile. "It's amazing how productive doing nothing can be."

"What?!" Sam cried. "That doesn't make any sense. We have to make a run for it!"

"What we have to do is slow down," his father insisted. "Clu has been growing exponentially more powerful. We're safe here in the Outlands. But as soon as we step onto that Grid . . . well, believe me, there's no move we can make that Clu hasn't already considered."

Kevin could see Sam was confused.

"In here, nothing happens unless Clu wants it to," Kevin said, trying to get his point across.

"That's not true," Sam said. "Look at us. We're here."

His father let out a deep sigh. "Tell me, Sam. What brought you to the Grid?"

"I told you," Sam replied. "Alan got a page from you."

"But I didn't send any page, Sam," Kevin said. "It was

Clu. This is all his design. He wanted a new piece on the board to change the game, and with you he got more than he ever dreamed. This is precisely what Clu wants. Us. Together. Heading for the Portal."

Kevin placed both hands on his son's shoulders. "It's Clu's game now, Sam," he said. "And the only way to win is not to play."

"That's a lousy way to live," Sam said through clenched teeth.

"Yes, but a way," his father said.

"We can go home!" Sam cried. "Don't you want that?"

Kevin was silent for a moment as he pondered his son's words. Finally, he spoke. "Sometimes life has a way of moving you past things like wants and hopes."

Sam didn't know what to say, what to do, to change his father's mind. But it didn't matter. The conversation seemed over.

"Quorra will show you to your room," said Kevin. "Good night, Sam."

Quorra led Sam into a wide, seemingly endless corridor.

"How can he be so afraid of his own creation?" Sam

asked her. "Dad built Clu. Why can't he end him?"

Quorra frowned. "He could, but it would require integration."

"All right, so why not—?"

"Your father would never survive the event," she explained. "It would be the end of them both."

"Well, I'm not sitting around here until some plan magically presents itself," Sam warned. "If Dad refuses to act, then I will."

"How?" Quorra whispered.

"I'm going through the Portal. Clu wants Dad's disc, not mine. Clu actually had my disc and handed it right back." Sam shook his head. "I'm going to get out. I'm going to find Alan Bradley, and we're going to figure this thing out on the other side. It might be Clu's game here, but in *my* world he's gone in a keystroke."

Sam clenched his fists. "Only I can't do anything until someone helps me get to the Portal. My gut tells me you don't want to be stuck here for eternity, either."

Quorra's eyes were wide. "I really think you should consider your father's wisdom," she argued.

"I have," said Sam.

After a long silence, Quorra gave Sam what looked like a business card. An odd symbol glowed in one corner. When Sam took the tiny plastic square, a holographic map appeared before his eyes.

"There's someone I once knew," Quorra said. "A program named Zuse, who fought alongside the ISOs. I haven't seen him in a long time, but they say he still runs the underground."

Sam studied the floating map.

"Zuse forges data for rogue programs, moves them around the Grid," Quorra explained. "They say he can get anyone anywhere."

"Then he can get me to the Portal," Sam said. "How do I find Zuse?"

Quorra pointed to a spot on the map. "This is his sector. Make it there alive and . . . he'll find you."

CHAPTER 6

SAM REVVED THE ENGINE ON HIS DAD'S LIGHT CYCLE. The chopper may have been vintage, but it moved. Which was good. Sam didn't have any time to waste. He had to get to Zuse.

Sam streaked a blazing path across the Outlands' ebony landscape. Everything except the skyline in the distance was carbon black. Sam focused on the flickering energy of the Grid's main city, glowing with unique particles of light.

As the lights grew brighter, Sam spotted a long, narrow bridge. He crossed it, entering into what Quorra told him was referred to as the Old City.

The streets were tangled and twisted here, but Sam didn't feel lost. This part of the city's digital metropolis was a reflection of the real one he'd lived in all his life. On the other hand, Sam noticed some disturbing differences.

This Old City showed more decay than the one back home. The roving Sentries and barbed wire looked wrong to Sam, too. But he recognized the layout well enough. He even knew that with a few turns he would be at his dad's arcade—or at least this digital domain's version of it.

"This is a restricted area," a metallic voice boomed through the dreary streets. "Authorized programs only. Violators without functionality or residence confirmation will be deleted. . . ."

Sam noticed Sentries up ahead. They were stopping passing programs and checking their disc IDs.

Better look for cover, Sam thought.

He ducked into an alley across from Flynn's arcade. As he parked his dad's cycle, he noticed a destitute program sleeping nearby. Sam traded his blue arena baton for the defeated program's ragged poncho. Disguised now, Sam ventured onto the main street.

"Sam Flynn?"

Turning, he recognized the pretty program approaching

him. This was the head Siren, the same living statue who had helped Sam suit up before he entered the arena. She looked more conventional now, wearing street clothes and carrying an umbrella.

"Do you remember me?" she asked.

Sam nodded. "You gave me some advice."

"And you followed it. I'm glad," the Siren said with a smile. "It's unfortunate we met the way we did."

"Yeah. Can I have my jeans back?" Sam asked.

"I am off duty now," the Siren replied.

"Well, you have a good night," he said, turning to go.

The Siren stopped him. "You're looking for someone?"

Sam froze. "What makes you say that?"

The Siren plucked Quorra's holographic card out of his hand. "Intuition," she replied flatly.

Just then, two armored Sentries appeared at the end of the block. The Siren pulled Sam into the shadows.

"I can help you, Sam Flynn," she whispered. "I know what you are looking for, and your other options don't strike me as particularly attractive." The Siren's gaze drifted to the Sentries.

Sam nodded once. The Siren took Sam's hand and led him away, out of the Old City and toward the new.

Back in the Outlands, Kevin awoke with a start. Sensing something was wrong, he got out of bed. In his bare feet he padded to where his son was supposed to be sleeping.

Sam was gone—and so was the vintage Light Cycle.

Kevin knew Sam could never have gotten out of the safe house without help. He summoned Quorra.

She found Kevin on the veranda staring out at the flickering lights of the metropolis. "The city is bright tonight," he said. "Clu is excited to see me."

Quorra flinched. *He knows I helped Sam. Did something happen?* The city lights *were* brighter than ever. Spotlight beams stabbed at the black sky. Quorra could see squadrons of air Sentries assembling above the city's towers.

Suddenly she became frightened. *Clu knew Sam was on the Grid! He was marshaling his forces.*

"Thank you for bringing my son to me," Kevin said quietly. Then he touched a button on his belt. Thick, plasma-laced armor morphed around him. Battle boots encased his bare feet.

The data disc Clu wanted appeared on Kevin's back. It glowed steadily in the shadowy light.

"You can't go," Quorra pleaded. "Sam is going to be okay. I sent him to someone we can trust."

But Kevin activated his faceplate. "I don't expect you to understand. There's no other choice."

Kevin's face looked almost ghostly inside the illuminated helmet. "Chaos," he said with a strange smile, looking at the flashing lights and assembling army. "That's *good* news."

<< >>

SAM FOLLOWED THE SIREN to a towering building. He craned his neck. The top of the building was pulsating with light. A symbol flashed in the brilliant neon. It was the same symbol he'd seen on Quorra's holographic data card.

Walking inside, Sam and the Siren boarded a glass elevator. She pressed the only button and the doors closed. The elevator soundlessly ran up the side of the colossal building. Sam marveled at the view. Not even the Encom Tower was as high as this monolith.

The elevator finally stopped. The doors opened and Sam's jaw dropped.

"What is this place?" he whispered.

The Siren took his hand. Her eyes were burning with a strange inner light. "This is the End of Line Club, Sam Flynn," she said. Then she tugged on Sam's hand, pulling him into the massive club.

The interior was vast and multileveled. Verandas, balconies—even floating islands—were crowded with programs. Helmeted DJs played music from a booth overlooking the kaleidoscopic floor.

The jam masters used color and light along with sound. Everything pulsated with different hues and shades. Even the programs changed color with the throbbing beat.

As Sam struggled to process this strange place, the Key Siren led him to the neon bar. They passed a row of Sentries sipping energy drinks. At the sight of the guards, Sam tensed with alarm.

"Relax," she said. "The Sentries are *occupied*."

She pointed out other Sirens just like her. They were sitting next to the Sentries, whispering to them.

Sam nodded and continued to follow the Siren. She led him to the base of a high platform at the center of the vast club. The platform was heavily guarded by grim-faced programs. They stood, arms folded and staring straight ahead, as the party flowed around them like ocean waves around giant boulders.

A man sat on the platform they were guarding. He wore a formal tailcoat and a top hat. He spun a cane in his left hand. His hair was white, his face the same pale color, and his clothes a startling white as well. He was like no program Sam had ever seen.

"His name is Castor," the Siren told Sam. "If you want to speak to Zuse, you have to go through him."

Sam noticed the wall of guards parting. A tough-looking program climbed the platform stairs. Pixels were missing in his face and neck—this world's version of a hideous scar.

"That's Bartik. Bartik the Anarchist," someone close to Sam whispered, pointing to his scarred face.

Bartik crossed the high platform and approached Castor. Down in the crowd, Bartik's gang watched the meeting with interest. So did Sam. He moved closer to hear what the two were saying.

"Have a sense of humor, my friend," Castor began. "It's only a revolution."

Plasma pulsated through Bartik's armor. "I didn't come here for entertainment," he snapped. "It's time. You can feel it. The boy's on the Grid. He's spurred hope."

Sam tensed. They were talking about him.

Bartik pointed to the windows. "The eastern sky is alight!"

Castor sighed. "And you wish me to ask Zuse to rally the troops? Stir the masses? Rouse the rabblers? Am I right?"

"Programs are disappearing, Castor," Bartik said. "Soon none of us will be left. We need to strike now. Unite the factions. Encourage revolution!"

"Of course, Zuse can do these things," Castor said, stifling a yawn.

"Then grant me an audience," Bartik pleaded.

Castor yawned deeply. "Your enthusiasm is intoxicating, dear Bartik, but Zuse's time is more than precious. We shall see. . . ."

The Siren turned to Sam. "Wait here."

He watched her move up the stairs. The guards never questioned her, and that surprised him. She leaned close to

Castor and whispered in his ear.

Castor glanced quickly at Sam, then took a harder look. Finally, he turned to Bartik and said, "If you'll excuse me a moment, I have to attend to something. But have a drink. Courtesy of End of Line."

Castor stepped down off the platform and walked right up to Sam. The programs around them suddenly got quiet. Sam felt like every program in the club was watching them, including Bartik and his gang. He wanted to shrink into his dirty poncho. But Castor hooked a thin arm around Sam's.

"Come away from these primitive functions," Castor cooed, leading him back onto the platform.

Castor glanced at him once more, his eyes filled with curiosity . . . and something else Sam couldn't pinpoint. "The Son of Flynn!" Castor gushed as they walked. "Of all the innumerable possibilities, of all the places he could have chosen, he just happens to walk into *mine*!"

CHAPTER 9

CASTOR LED SAM AND THE SIREN to his private table in the massive nightclub.

"Libations! Quickly!" Castor called to a waiter. Then he slid his scarecrowlike physique into the seat beside Sam. Smiling, Castor lifted his top hat and extended his hand.

"Castor, your host," he said. "Provider of any and all diversions. At your service."

Sam got right to the point. "I'm looking for Zuse."

Castor arched an eyebrow. "Indeed. Many are. . . ."

"Where can I find him?"

Castor glanced at the crowd. Everyone was watching. Everyone was listening. All of them pretended they weren't.

"This, good sir, is a conversation best had behind closed doors," Castor said, rising. "Perhaps we should adjourn to the *private* lounge?"

Castor waved his hand, dismissing the Siren. But as Sam was hustled away, he called to her over his shoulder.

"Thank you—" Sam paused, not knowing the Siren's true name.

"Gem," she told him. "My name is Gem."

Then, before Sam could say more, Castor hustled him off the platform and through the crowd. They paused when they arrived under the elevated booth that housed the club's DJs. Castor spoke to them briefly.

"I'm slipping away for a moment, boys," he said, waving a lazy hand to encompass the club. "*Change* the scheme. *Alter* the *mood*, would you be so kind?"

Castor tapped his cane to slow the music's beat. The DJs responded. The club darkened. The color scheme changed.

The blue waves of plasma running along the walls now pulsed in a deep purple. Soon the entire building throbbed with a purple glow, both inside and out.

Castor smiled with satisfaction. Then he tapped the floor one last time.

Sam jumped backward when a section of the ground opened. An ornate spiral staircase emerged from the pit. The staircase spun like a drill bit as it shot upward. Finally it stopped.

"Whoa," Sam whispered.

"Designed it myself," Castor boasted. "Elegant, no?"

<< >>

MEANWHILE, IN THE CARBON-BLACK OUTLANDS, Clu had arrived at Kevin's safe house. It had taken longer than anticipated and he was anxious. Not that he would admit that—ever. He moved onto the veranda and took in the view from Flynn's mountaintop. Then he strode back inside and scanned the living quarters.

"Cozy," Clu said.

Right now, his Sentries were searching the compound, eager to find Kevin as quickly as possible.

Clu continued to look around the area, and his gaze landed on the dining room table. He picked up an apple from the fruit bowl and wondered at its purpose. Such strange things in this place. What need did Kevin have for them? His thoughts were interrupted when Jarvis entered. The counselor was flanked by the Black Guard—Clu's private army—in dark, faceless armor.

"Our Sentries discovered Flynn's outmoded Light Cycle in the Old City," Jarvis reported. "I assure you, we traced its energy signature back to this place. But Flynn must have fled before we arrived."

Clu glanced at his own reflection in a giant mirror, his mind racing back to that moment when Kevin first created him.

"You are Clu," Flynn had said. "You are to create the perfect system. Together, we're going to change the world."

Clu had never disobeyed Kevin's first command.

It was Flynn who lost his way, Clu thought. Flynn chose flaws over the flawless—the ISOs instead of perfection. . . .

Just then, Clu noticed Flynn's chessboard. Enraged, he swept it clean.

"Leader," Jarvis said nervously, "might I direct your attention to the End of Line Club?"

Clu peered through the room's arched windows. On the distant skyline, Clu noticed that the tower was pulsing with purple light. For the first time that evening, Clu smiled.

MEANWHILE, BACK IN THE CITY, Sam and Castor were ascending the club's spiral staircase.

Castor's private lounge was located high above the End of Line Club's dance floor. The lounge's ceiling, floor, and walls were all glass, and the room was bathed in the same purple glow that lit the rest of the club.

"You can't be too careful," Castor said. "You've caused quite a stir with your arrival. Whispers of revolution are gaining volume. The Grid is alight."

Castor offered Sam a chair. "Zuse has been around since the earliest days of the Grid," he continued. "To survive, he had to mind all the percentages, all the angles."

"So when do I meet him?" Sam asked.

Castor bowed his head. "You just did."

Sam blinked. He hadn't seen that coming. "*You're* Zuse?"

"After the Purge, I needed to reinvent myself," Zuse explained. "Self preservation, you understand. Now, what can I do for you?"

"I need to get to the Portal," Sam said.

Zuse pointed his cane at a light shining on the horizon. "The spire to the east, as I'm sure you're aware. It's quite a journey. Beyond the far reaches of the Outlands and across the Sea of Simulation."

"Then you can help me?" Sam asked.

"Of course," Zuse replied. "But first, tell me. Have you seen . . . *him*?"

Sam knew Zuse was asking about his dad, but he said nothing.

After a moment, Zuse nodded. "You're a man who understands the value of information. I should expect no less from a Flynn. At least tell me who sent you to me."

"Her name's Quorra," Sam said. "She said she knew you a long time ago."

"Indeed she did," Zuse said. "Many cycles ago. It was a different time. But let's not relive the past. Let's worry about your future."

Zuse laid a friendly hand on Sam's shoulder. He frowned at the ragged poncho. "We'll need to change your attire," he said. "And you'll need a forged disc. And of course you'll need transport across the Sea of Simulation."

Zuse spun his cane and laughed. "This is going to be quite the ride!"

For the first time since he'd entered the Grid, Sam felt himself relaxing. He reached for the drink that Zuse offered him. But as he did so, he glanced up through the glass skylight. His heart pounded.

Four members of the Black Guard were bearing down toward him on high-tech parachutes!

It's a trap! Sam realized. He glared at the program across the table. Zuse just shrugged.

"I believed in users once before," he grimly confessed. "But the game has changed, Son of Flynn."

Sam had to act quickly. Dropping his drink, he ran to the spiral staircase. But the steps were gone! Beneath Sam's feet, a sea of dancers swayed to the trancelike rhythms.

Just then, the skylight above Sam exploded, fracturing into pixilated shards. A Guard came down right on top of him!

The air left Sam's lungs with a *whoosh*. As he grappled with his foe, they both tumbled through the open door. Then Sam and the Guard plunged toward the dance floor below!

CHAPTER 10

PATRONS SCATTERED WHEN SAM and the Guard slammed onto the top of the long bar. Drinks flew and glass shattered. Luckily, Sam turned around during the fall. The Guard landed first, absorbing most of the impact. But the armored Guard still fought!

Sam snatched a long-necked bottle and bashed the Guard over the head. The Guard's helmet shattered, and he derezzed with a sizzle.

As Sam rolled off the bar, more Black Guard soldiers landed on the dance floor. The bouncers drew their discs and fired at the Guards. Dozens of shots were deflected, but a few unlucky dancers were derezzed by ricochets. The Guards fired back as complete chaos erupted.

Apparently undisturbed by all the action, the DJs simply sped up the beat. But no one was dancing. Freaked-out programs stampeded for the exit. Other terrified programs huddled against the walls or dived under tables.

One voice rang out above all the chaotic noise. "Resist!"

It was Bartik. The Anarchist was rallying his troops. They pulled their weapons free, and more deadly discs began criss-crossing the crowded club.

Within moments, a Guard was derezzed. His fellow Guards closed ranks and advanced. From behind the bar, Sam was about to cry out a warning, but it was too late.

With ruthless efficiency the Guards eliminated Bartik's gang. Now only the leader remained.

A Guard stepped forward and hurled his disc. Bartik grabbed an attractive young program and used her for a shield. She derezzed with a scream. Then two discs struck the Anarchist at the same time. Bartik burst into a flurry of bouncing cubes.

Time to go, Sam decided. Crouching low, he started moving toward the nearest exit. Then he heard a thump and looked up.

Zuse stood on the bar, staring down at Sam and cackling. He pointed his cane, and Sam was pinned in a spotlight beam.

"Behold the Son of Flynn!" Zuse shouted. "Behold the son of our maker!"

Like heat-seeking missiles, Black Guard moved in for the kill. Any hapless program that got in their way was ruthlessly derezzed.

As Sam once again made a move for the exit, a member of the Black Guard tossed his disc. The aim was true. The disc's gleaming edge was about to kill Sam when—

KEL-LACK!

Another disc expertly deflected the first. Then it bounced off the DJ booth and smoothly returned to its owner.

It was Quorra! With graceful ease, she caught her disc, then strode into the center of the room. Immediately, she deflected another shot. With a perfectly aimed ricochet, she derezzed the Black Guard who'd almost killed Sam.

Zuse danced along the top of the bar, grooving on the DJ's sound. Quorra shot him an accusing look. Zuse responded with a mad laugh.

Joining Quorra, Sam deflected a disc aimed at her back. He wanted to thank her, but there was no time.

Quorra plowed through the Guards, taking them out one

by one. Her moves were graceful and elegant. Quorra used her baton defensively and derezzed opponents only if forced to. She clearly had experience with this sort of thing.

Sam's style of fighting was much rawer. Using his disc, he eliminated any Guard that got in his way. But his anger made him reckless—a weakness in battle. Fortunately, the exit was now in sight.

Suddenly, from out of nowhere, a Guard lunged for him. The Guard raised his disc like a battle-ax. At the last moment, Quorra jumped between Sam and the descending disc. The razor-sharp edge cut through her upraised arm. In a burst of blue energy, her arm was severed.

No! Sam derezzed the Guard with a quick slash of his disc. Then he lifted Quorra. Her eyes were fluttering. A strange glow suffused the stump of her arm.

Behind Sam, a disc bounced off the wall. He looked up. A half-dozen Black Guardsmen were closing in on him! Behind them, Zuse kept up his crazy dancing.

Sam waited for the end.

But the end didn't come. . . .

Blue lightning did.

Like an airborne power surge, the electricity crackled through the club. Programs screamed as sparks exploded from the walls and floor. Then, eerily, the lightning collected itself, forming a whirling plasma cloud. With a flash of raw power, it shorted out all the purple lights—and knocked out every last Black Guardsman. Their armor clattered as the dark, hulking programs hit the floor.

A familiar hand touched Sam's shoulder.

"Stay with me," his father said.

When the surviving programs saw the face of Sam's dad, they began to murmur. Every last one of them recognized their creator. They cleared a path for Kevin, allowing him to pass.

Sam followed his father out of the club, carrying Quorra in his arms. His dad held open the doors of the glass elevator and Sam moved inside quickly.

But back in the club, several of the Black Guard were already recovering. One stumbled to his feet. As Kevin stepped into the elevator, the guard fired a grappling hook. With a clank, the hook snagged the disc on Kevin's back!

A split second before the elevator doors shut, the Guard yanked the cord. Kevin's disc flew into the Guard's hands.

Unaware of what had just happened, Sam hit the button and the elevator began to descend. It was only then that Kevin reached back and realized his disc was gone. The loss sent him staggering into the corner, speechless.

Back in the club, another Guard fired a grenade at the elevator. The explosion blew the doors off and cut the cable. The elevator began to drop! Sam punched every button in sight, but the car only picked up speed!

"Hello!" Sam yelled. "A little help here!"

The sound of his son's cry brought Kevin back to life. With one lift of his hand, a control panel appeared in the glass wall of the car. Kevin's fingers flew across a crystalline keypad.

Sam looked down at Quorra in his arms. She was unconscious. Her arm stump continued to bleed energy.

Flynn's actions weren't helping. If anything, the elevator was plunging faster, despite the man's frantic efforts.

Holding Quorra close, Sam braced for impact.

CHAPTER 11

SAM REFUSED TO CLOSE HIS EYES. In just a few more seconds, the elevator would slam into the street.

Suddenly Kevin whooped in triumph. At the last possible moment, the concrete opened up. The elevator car continued its descent down, and then *through*, the city street!

The glass car dropped through sublevel after sublevel. The underground world was stacked with acres of maintenance machinery, networks of pipes, and ribbons of cables.

Plasma energy throbbed through grid lines embedded in the walls. These glowing conduits were the underground world's sole source of light. Their radiant energy powered the machines that kept the city running.

Finally the elevator plunged into a dark tube and slowed to a stop. When the doors opened, Sam lifted Quorra out. Trying to still his own shaking legs and slow his beating heart, he stepped out onto a platform, his eyes growing wide. They had gone much farther than he thought. In front of him was the Sea of Simulation.

Massive wharves stretched as far as the eye could see. The structures floated in a blue-black ether. Beyond the docks, a fleet of vehicles he recognized as solar sailers hung in the digital sky, their winglike panels folded.

Sam realized the winged sailers were tied to floating cargo containers. While he watched, one hovering ship spread its massive wing panels. The sailer pulled away from the dock, towing a container as large as a skyscraper.

As Kevin moved to join his son, Sam finally saw the empty sheath on his back.

"Are you all right?" Sam asked with worry, his father's earlier behavior now understandable. "Your disc. It's gone."

"It is," Kevin replied.

"And that's a *big* problem, right?" Sam asked.

His dad raised an eyebrow. "Is it?"

Sam looked down at the unconscious woman in his arms. "I'm sorry," he said. "I know I screwed up, but we can go back—"

His father shook his head slightly. "This is the road we're on now," Kevin said. "We head to the east. To the Portal. Unless something else happens . . ."

Kevin moved down a series of ramps to reach the docks. Sam stayed right behind him, carrying Quorra.

The piers were stacked with machinery and cargo. But there were no programs there. The cargo loaders and ships didn't need programs because they were all automated.

Sam followed his father onto a long, rising catwalk. The incline led right up to one of the larger solar sailers hovering in the air. The two boarded the flying ship, and Kevin ducked into the bridge. He easily overrode the navigational system and quickly entered his own coordinates.

Sam stood on the deck as the ship's sails unfurled. With a high-pitched whine, the solar sailer linked to a beam of plasma high in the sky. Riding this tide of power, the ship could travel all the way across the Sea of Simulation.

"This ship knows the way now," Kevin said, joining his son on deck. "It will take us to the Portal. . . ."

WITH RINZLER BY HIS SIDE, Clu found Zuse at his shattered club. Still in top hat and tails, Zuse twirled a cane in one hand and Kevin's disc in the other.

There was no sign of the Black Guardsmen that Clu had dispatched to take out the Flynns.

Derezzed, no doubt, Clu mused. So Zuse could seize Flynn's disc for himself. Clu did not express his thoughts aloud, however.

"The boy and Flynn are gone?" Clu asked.

Zuse shrugged. "I presume, Your Excellency, that they perished in the elevator."

"You *presume*?" Clu sneered behind his visor. Then he whirled to face his black-armored enforcer.

"Rinzler, go!" Clu commanded.

The elite guard turned on his heels and marched to the destroyed elevator. Meanwhile, dozens of guards entered the club to replace him.

Zuse made a point of ignoring Clu's show of force. Clu pretended to ignore the disc in the club owner's hand.

"So you saw Flynn," Clu said. "How's he look?"

"Aged," Zuse replied. "And my apologies for not delivering the entire package. I pride myself on execution, but when Kevin Flynn entered, everything changed. The programs became unpredictable."

Zuse paused, recalling the response Flynn got from the crowd. "I've never seen anything like it," he said. "Their awe was palpable. . . ."

"Right," said Clu. "Now, about that disc."

Zuse rolled the disc down his cane until it was within Clu's reach. But when Clu went to snatch it, Zuse rolled it back again.

"I presume our understanding is still valid," Zuse said. "Control of the city?"

"You'll get the reward you deserve," Clu replied. Behind him, the Black Guard busily moved through the club.

"A sizable request, I know." Zuse displayed the disc in his hand. "But how long have you been searching for this? Over a thousand cycles, no? Imagine the secrets this disc holds, the master key to all the riddles of the universe—"

"Give it to me!" Clu commanded.

Zuse glanced at the Guards. At the sound of their leader's raised voice, they had taken a step closer. Zuse knew there was no more negotiating. He handed the disc to Clu.

"I realize our alliance is at times uneasy, Clu, but always necessary," Zuse hastily said.

Why are they still advancing? Zuse wondered.

Clu wasn't paying attention to the club owner any longer. His gaze was transfixed by the disc in his hand.

Zuse swallowed, nervous now. "You know you need me right where I am, Clu," he said.

"You're right," Clu replied with a little smile. He snapped his fingers. The Black Guard closed in. Before Zuse could escape, they restrained him and bound him to a chair with powerful force bands.

Clu started for the exit. "Enjoy your club while you have it, Zuse," he called over his shoulder. "And don't ever presume. . . ."

Fully panicked now, Zuse struggled against the restraints. But it was useless. The Black Guard turned and marched away, falling in behind their leader. That's when Zuse noticed the bundles of explosives wired to his club's bar and DJ booths.

On a nearby table, a small digital display ticked down the seconds before detonation. His eyes widened with fear.

This was the end for the End of Line Club—and for Zuse.

<< >>

OUT ON THE SEA OF SIMULATION, a devastating flash lit up the horizon. The blinding brightness made Sam squint. Shock waves rippled through the ozone. The echoing boom rolled all the way across the blue-black water.

Sam turned back and gawked at the city skyline. A piece of it was glowing red now. Like a Roman candle, the End of Line Club burned hot and fast before the entire building beneath it collapsed.

"Clu?" Sam whispered.

His dad nodded.

Sam clenched his fist. "What's he doing?"

Kevin did not answer. Instead he went and kneeled beside Quorra. His father took her disc in his hands and began to manipulate it.

Finally Kevin looked back at Sam.

"He wants a little fresh air," Kevin explained. "Clu is done with this place."

"Him getting *out*? To our world?" Sam shook his head. "Dad, it doesn't seem possible."

"It is possible," his father said matter-of-factly. He was still working on Quorra's disc.

"But you created everything in here. Every program, every place!"

Kevin tapped the empty sheath on his spine, where the disc had been. "Like I said. Golden ticket."

A holograph suddenly flickered above Quorra's disc. Kevin frowned. This was not good. Her vital signs were failing.

Sam saw the worry on his father's face. "Is she going to make it?"

"I don't know," he replied softly. "I have to identify the damaged code. The sequencing. It's enormously complex."

He concentrated, worked a few more minutes, and finally cracked the code. The disc opened like a makeup compact. Light flooded the bridge of the sailer with kaleidoscopic torrents of color.

"She risked herself for me. . . ." The realization weighed on Sam.

"Some things are worth the risk," Kevin assured his son. Then his eyes went wide. "Hey, look at that!"

Sam watched a holographic grid appear where Quorra's arm used to be. The limb became a glowing mass. Then pixels began to re-form around the grid lines.

"Now that's impressive, if I do say so myself," Kevin said, with the hint of a smile.

"She's going to be all right now?" Sam asked.

"It will take a little while for her system to reboot, but yes. She'll be fine." Kevin exhaled and a full grin finally spread across his bearded face. "Nothing like a little bio-digital regeneration to move the spirit, eh?"

He slapped his son's back.

CHAPTER 12

FROM THE DECK OF THE FLOATING SOLAR SHIP, Kevin watched the digital sky as his son filled him in on what was going on in his world.

". . . And there's a war in the Middle East, and the Lakers and Celtics are still at it," Sam went on. "The rich are getting richer. The poor are getting poorer. We have cell phones. There's online dating, and Wi-Fi—"

"Why-Fly?" Kevin interrupted, an eyebrow raised.

"Wi-Fi," Sam repeated slowly. "Wireless Interlinking—"

"Of digital devices? I thought of that in 1979!" Kevin cried with indignation.

Sam shrugged. It didn't really surprise him. Then he

remembered one more thing. "Hey, remember your Ducati motorcycle?"

His father smiled and nodded. "Not a day goes by I don't think about that bike."

"I'm fixing her up," Sam said proudly.

"I didn't realize she was broken," Kevin said.

Sam put his hand on his dad's shoulder. "Twenty years in a garage, no tarp. She needed a little love."

"How's she run?"

"I'll let you know when I get her out there," Sam said.

"Man," Kevin said with a faraway gaze. "I'd like to see that."

"You will," Sam promised.

For a moment, father and son were lost in thoughts of rebuilding their family. Then they both heard a groan. Quorra was waking up.

"Here," Kevin said, handing Sam a flask. "Give her this."

Sam helped Quorra take a sip. His father moved off, his gaze fixed to the eastern sky.

"Time for me to knock on the sky and listen to the sound," Kevin said cryptically as he walked away.

RINZLER STRODE AMONG THE CRATES and cargo-loading machines on the crowded dock. Like a digital bloodhound, he sensed his creator's presence.

Rinzler knew he was close.

The enforcer paused at one pier. Not far now, he thought. A few more strides brought him to an access bridge. The rising catwalk led to nothing but empty sky.

They left on a solar ship that was moored right here, Rinzler realized. He touched the catwalk and the structure crackled. Ripples of energy spread outward. The corrosive power shorted out loaders and dimmed lights.

Rinzler lifted a hand. Instruments built into his gauntlet summoned the U-shaped Recognizer hovering overhead. The massive machine settled onto the dock. Rinzler boarded.

On the bridge, he punched in new navigational coordinates. The Recognizer lifted off a few seconds later. With an electronic hum the airship headed east, out over the Sea of Simulation.

QUORRA SNATCHED THE FLASK from Sam's hand and drained it dry. Then she looked around, confused.

"We're safe now," Sam explained, "headed east, toward the Portal."

But Quorra frowned. "Clu has the disc?"

"Yes," Sam said. "But once I get out, I can shut him down."

"I *never* should have sent you to Zuse. It was a mistake," she said softly.

Sam touched her arm. "It's okay. I've made a few myself."

Quorra looked doubtful. "Where did Flynn go?" she asked.

Sam scratched his head. "I *think* he's knocking on the sky—"

Quorra finished Sam's thought. "And listening to the sound."

"You've heard that one before?" Sam asked.

"I've heard them all," Quorra answered. "I've been with him a long time."

On the other side of the deck, Kevin had returned from

whatever he had been doing and was sitting in a lotus position. He suddenly stirred.

"I haven't seen him this way in a long time," Quorra said quietly, gazing at him.

Sam shook his head wonderingly. "What happened to him?"

"He lost hope," Quorra replied.

"Of defeating Clu?"

Quorra shook her head. "Of getting out. Of seeing *you*, Sam."

Just then, the two became aware of a dazzling sight on the eastern horizon. A massive pillar of brilliance reached into the black sky. Though it was nearly blinding to stare at, neither Sam nor Quorra could tear their gazes away.

The Portal . . .

"What a view," Sam whispered.

Quorra nodded. "The Portal used to tell us that Flynn was here. It became a symbol of something bigger, something better than this world."

Quorra shielded her eyes. "I've never been this close to the Portal before. It's how I imagine a sunrise to be."

Sam glanced at the single-hued glow. Mentally, he measured it against the splendor of a real sunrise.

"Trust me," he said. "There's no comparison."

"What's it like?" Quorra asked.

"The sun? Oh, man . . . I've never described it." He gazed intently at Quorra. "Warm. Radiant. Beautiful."

Suddenly Kevin appeared. "Get below! Move!" he cried.

Sam rose and followed his dad's gaze. There, lurking in the distance, he saw the square lines of a Recognizer. The ship quickly vanished behind a black mountain. But not before Quorra saw it, too.

They scanned the rugged peak that rose above the Sea of Simulation like an island in an ocean. Soon the Recognizer reappeared. The craft was approaching their ship!

The deck under their feet suddenly shuddered. Sam watched a bright tractor beam reach out from the Recognizer. It caught the solar sailer's plasma stream and bent it to alter their course. Now their ship was headed for an island Sam had seen out of the corner of his eye a few moments before.

Quorra grabbed Sam's arm and dragged him down to the cargo hold. Sam peered through a porthole. The sails were retracting. The ship was preparing to dock.

"What happened?" Sam asked.

"A new course," his dad said, coming to join them.

The sailer entered a mammoth cave in the face of the mountainside. The cargo bay was plunged into darkness. Sam stared as sheer rock walls slid past the window. Then he heard Quorra gasp.

In the darkness, the cargo containers began to glow, and Sam could make out their contents. The containers were packed with programs. Thousands of them. Frozen. Inert. Locked inside some sort of electronic trance. They were stacked one on top of the other.

"What is this?" Quorra asked.

"Clu can't create programs," Kevin explained. "He can only destroy or repurpose them."

"Repurpose them for what?" Quorra asked in alarm.

"Look here," Sam called from the porthole. He had just seen the answer to Quorra's question.

The ship had entered a massive underground facility in the heart of the mountain. The cave was filled with Sentries and Black Guardsmen. Soldier programs stood in rigid ranks. All wore identical uniforms and carried war discs on their backs.

Another sprawling sector held thousands of armored tanks.

They were larger than the tanks in the Tron game. All of them had rotating turrets with two cannons mounted on their beetle black hulls.

"Clu is building an invasion army," Sam said grimly.

And it wasn't hard for him to guess which world Clu was planning to invade.

CHAPTER 17

SAM, KEVIN, AND QUORRA SLIPPED OUT of the cargo bay after their ship docked. The automatic loaders began working on the towed container, which gave them a chance to escape. Whatever had pulled them in here did not yet know of their existence.

Or so they thought.

As soon as they stepped onto the dock, Sam spotted trouble.

Rinzler was striding down the dock. Behind him, Clu's throne ship hovered like a vulture eager to dive on its prey.

Rinzler homed in on Quorra, his pace increasing. She gasped. Fear momentarily shadowed her features. Then a quiet calm came over her as she accepted her fate. Sam stepped forward to face him. Meanwhile, Quorra detached her disc and handed it to Kevin.

"They can't know you're here," she said calmly, and then she whispered, "Good-bye."

"You don't have to do this," Kevin said.

But Quorra took off. With preternatural speed, she bolted and then leaped on top of the cargo crates. Rinzler followed. But Quorra moved so fast Rinzler couldn't catch her.

Jumping from crate to crate, Quorra headed for the throne ship. When she hit the access ladder on the ship's outer skin, she climbed the rungs to reach the airship's upper deck. Then she shattered the ladder with her baton so Rinzler couldn't follow.

When he saw that the ladder had shattered, Rinzler paused— but just for a moment. Then the enforcer drew the disc from his back and split it.

He leaped onto the hull of the Rectifier. With a metallic clang, he plunged the discs into the vessel's hull. Using the disc's sharp edges the way a mountaineer would use spikes, he climbed all the way up to the bridge.

Sam watched helplessly as Rinzler overtook Quorra.

"We can't just let her go!" Sam cried as Quorra was dragged into the Rectifier.

"We have no other choice," Kevin said. "Come on!"

Sam followed his father to the end of the docking bay. They were in the off-loading zone now. Programs awaiting processing were stacked like fireplace logs.

Sam watched while a huge, spinning wheel emerged from the ground. A conveyor belt began feeding programs into the wheel's path. The whirling disc held them and then twirled each program once. Then it spit them out on the other side, each program now clad in identical military uniforms and armed with a war disc.

"It's a reeducation chamber," Kevin said in horror.

"And Quorra's going to wind up like one of them if we don't save her," Sam pointed out. They had to do something. Now.

<< >>

CLU STOOD ON THE Rectifier's hangar deck. He was about to address his elite Black Guard when Rinzler interrupted.

Annoyed by the distraction, Clu faced his enforcer. He was surprised to find that Rinzler had a prisoner.

"Where's your disc?"

Quorra's silence was his answer. Clu touched her cheek with a gloved hand. "Where is Flynn?"

She still said nothing.

"Never mind. I have something special in mind for you." Clu pushed Quorra aside to address Rinzler. "Take her away. And find *them*."

Rinzler seized Quorra's arm.

"I've seen what users are capable of," Quorra cried. "You don't belong with them, Clu!"

Clu ignored her furious charges. When Quorra was gone, he composed himself and ascended the podium. Rumbling cheers from his elite Black Guard greeted Clu. He began to speak.

"Together we have achieved many things," Clu said. "We've built a new world. Created a vast and complex system. Maintained it. Improved it. Rid it of its imperfections!"

Rousing cheers greeted Clu's words.

"Not to mention rid it of the false deity who sought to enslave us . . ." Clu paused and smirked as he raised his eyes skyward. "Kevin Flynn, *where are you now*?!"

Hidden away, Kevin heard Clu's cry. He was dying to answer his treacherous creation. But he remained silent. He knew they had to stay hidden if they wanted to continue living.

Unfortunately, the more Clu talked, the more difficult it was for Kevin to listen. Clu's voice sounded like his own voice. Clu's face looked like his own face. But the words that echoed up from the hangar were not his words or his thoughts. They were twisted conclusions from a corrupted mind, full of arrogance and hatred. They had *nothing* to do with Kevin's vision. . . .

Or did they? he found himself wondering. After all, I created Clu. Is some part of me like him?

"There was a time I believed this was all there was, all we were capable of," Clu declared as he continued to lecture his troops. "But I'm here to tell you that you've been kept in the dark too long."

Clu raised his hands. "Fellow programs, let there be no doubt. Our world is a cage no more. The key to the next frontier is finally in our possession!"

Clu gestured to a point a few decks above where Sam and his father hid. A light appeared, illuminating the ship's bridge. Kevin's disc was up there. Clu had mounted it on a high-tech pedestal as if it were a sacred object.

The disc was glowing. Active. Ready to lead Clu and his army through the portal and out into the real world.

"Unlike our selfish creator, I will make Flynn's world open and available to us all!" Clu bellowed. "In that world, our systems will grow. There our systems will blossom!"

Clu raised his hands over his head. "Together, we have changed this world. Together, we can change the *new* world, too. So I ask you. Are you ready to receive your command?"

The massive Black Guard army nodded in unison. "Yes!"

"Maximize efficiency," Clu commanded. "Rid the new system of imperfection! Rid the new system of the *users*!"

Cheers erupted from the Black Guard. The vibrations were loud enough to shake the catwalk under Sam's boots.

Sam exchanged a horrified glance with his father. Rid the new system of its users, Sam thought. But "users" are humans.

Clu wants to rid the world of people!

"WE *HAVE* TO GET YOUR DISC!" Sam whispered, feeling almost frantic now. He pointed above them, to the shining object displayed on the ship's bridge.

"No," Kevin quietly replied, refusing to even look at it. "We must beat Clu to the Portal. You can shut him down from the outside."

But Sam pointed out the army assembled below them. "Even if I make it out, by the time I find Alan Bradley, you'll be long gone," Sam said. "The disc is the only way!"

Kevin considered his son's words.

"Come on, Dad. We can do this."

But once again Kevin shook his head. "If we go now, at

least maybe *you* can get out. At least there's a chance."

"What about everything you created?" Sam asked.

"It's just a program, Sam!" his father responded, finally losing his cool. "It can all be rewritten. You can't. It's not worth your life."

"What about you? What about Quorra?" Sam asked. "You said it yourself, Dad. Some things are worth the risk."

Kevin blinked in surprise. His own words had come back to haunt him.

"I'm not going back alone, Dad."

Before his dad could argue, Sam took off toward the bridge— and his father's disc.

<< >>

THE MOMENT SAM EXITED THE ELEVATOR, he was attacked by two Sentries. He hurled his disc at one, derezzing him instantly.

The other swung his disc. But Sam ducked in time and gripped the Sentry's legs. With a heave, he tossed the armored guard over the rail.

Three more Sentries appeared. A warrior in action, Sam quickly reduced them to pixels. Then he crossed the bridge and stood before the pedestal. The disc glowed with an inner radiance. But as Sam reached for it, Counselor Jarvis rose in front of him.

"Stop!" Jarvis shouted.

Sam raised his disc with threatening fury, and the cowardly program shrank backward.

"At least I can say I *tried* to stop him," Jarvis muttered to himself.

Sam returned to the pedestal. But he was back in Jarvis's face a moment later. "I came with a girl—a program," he said. "*Where* is she?"

A door opened. Sam saw Quorra standing there. He rushed forward to meet her.

That's what Rinzler was waiting for—he stepped out of the shadows, surprising Sam.

"Sam! Go!" Quorra shouted.

Instead, Sam faced Rinzler. Dropping into a crouch, he reached behind him with his left hand while he raised his disc with his right.

Rinzler drew his own disc and split it. With a quick flick of his arm, he fired off the first. The toss was aimed directly at Sam's head.

Sam deflected the first throw with his own disc, but the move left his torso exposed.

Rinzler smiled as he shot his second disc. The razor-sharp edge was coming right for Sam! He was going to be cut in two!

That's when Sam brought his left hand forward. It was holding his dad's disc!

Sam knocked aside Rinzler's second throw. Then he sent his dad's disc ricocheting off the ship's hull. The attack surprised the enforcer. He had no time to react.

The sharp edge of Kevin's disc struck Rinzler square in the chest. Pieces of his thick armor broke off and derezzed. Rinzler howled as the force sent him backward, over the bridge rail.

Sam put up his hand, snagging his father's boomeranging disc in midair. Then he sheathed it beside his own and went to Quorra.

She threw her arms around Sam and squeezed him

tightly. "Thank you," she whispered.

"Let's go," Sam said, pullingggg awayandsnatching some familiarfamiliar

Equip00011111ment fr00000000m

Aaaaa00000001101010001000

011100101011001

N0e1rb10y r0a0c0k

0100101001

1110001001

011

00111 System Error . . .

FATAL ERROR

To reboot and recover lost data, scan below.

⟨⟨ If scan fails, visit http://disneybooks.com/tron ⟩⟩

⟨⟨ If issue persists, contact your systems administrator. ⟩⟩